Dear Parents:

Congratulations! Your child is taking the first steps on an exciting journey. The destination? Independent reading!

STEP INTO READING® will help your child get there. The program offers five steps to reading success. Each step includes fun stories and colorful art or photographs. In addition to original fiction and books with favorite characters, there are Step into Reading Non-Fiction Readers, Phonics Readers and Boxed Sets, Sticker Readers, and Comic Readers—a complete literacy program with something to interest every child.

Learning to Read, Step by Step!

Ready to Read   Preschool–Kindergarten
• big type and easy words • rhyme and rhythm • picture clues
For children who know the alphabet and are eager to begin reading.

Reading with Help   Preschool–Grade 1
• basic vocabulary • short sentences • simple stories
For children who recognize familiar words and sound out new words with help.

Reading on Your Own   Grades 1–3
• engaging characters • easy-to-follow plots • popular topics
For children who are ready to read on their own.

Reading Paragraphs   Grades 2–3
• challenging vocabulary • short paragraphs • exciting stories
For newly independent readers who read simple sentences with confidence.

Ready for Chapters   Grades 2–4
• chapters • longer paragraphs • full-color art
For children who want to take the plunge into chapter books but still like colorful pictures.

STEP INTO READING® is designed to give every child a successful reading experience. The grade levels are only guides; children will progress through the steps at their own speed, developing confidence in their reading.

Remember, a lifetime love of reading starts with a single step!

Step into Reading, Random House, and the Random House colophon are registered trademarks of Penguin Random House LLC.

Visit us on the Web!
StepIntoReading.com
rhcbooks.com

Educators and librarians, for a variety of teaching tools, visit us at RHTeachersLibrarians.com

ISBN 978-0-7364-4026-4 (trade) — ISBN 978-0-7364-8283-7 (lib. bdg.)
ISBN 978-0-7364-4027-1 (ebook)

Printed in the United States of America 10 9 8 7 6 5 4 3

DISNEP

FROZEN II

Elsa's Epic Journey

by Susan Amerikaner

illustrated by the Disney Storybook Art Team

Random House New York

Long ago,
Anna and Elsa's mother
sang them a song
about a secret river.
The river held the
answers to questions
about the past.

Now Elsa and Anna
are grown up.
Their parents are gone.
But they still have each other.

Elsa has many questions.

She wants to know why

she has a magic power.

She hears a voice

calling to her.

She thinks the voice

knows the answers.

Elsa's power grows.

She lets out an icy blast.

The trolls arrive.

They tell Elsa

that her power

woke the spirits

of the Enchanted Forest.

The voice calling to Elsa
tells her to go north.
Elsa listens to it.

Anna, Kristoff, Olaf,
and Sven go with her.
They find the
Enchanted Forest.

The friends meet
the Wind Spirit.
It helps Elsa
use her power
in a new way.

Elsa and her friends

meet the Northuldra

and some Arendellian soldiers.

Elsa meets

Honeymaren and Ryder.

Elsa and Anna learn that

the Northuldra

are more like them

than they are different.

They also meet an
Arendellian soldier
named Mattias,
who was friends
with their father.

Suddenly, a Fire Spirit
sets the area aflame!
Elsa tries to stop
the fire with her power.

Mattias shares stories
about Anna's father
when he was young.

Elsa and Honeymaren

become friends.

They talk about

the spirits.

Elsa, Anna, and Olaf
continue the journey.
Kristoff and Sven
stay behind.
The sisters
find an old shipwreck.

It is their parents' ship!
Their parents
were searching
for the secret river.
They wanted to know
why Elsa has magic.

Elsa must also find
the special river.
She knows her journey
will be very dangerous.

Elsa wants to protect
Anna and Olaf.
She sends them to safety
on an ice boat.

Lisa keeps moving north.

She reaches the Dark Sea.

She must cross it

to continue.

The Water Nokk

tries to stop Elsa.

It cannot beat her.

She cannot beat it.

They realize they

are equals.

Anna and Olaf

enter a cave.

An ice sculpture appears

in front of them.

It is a message

from Elsa, telling Anna

what she needs to do

to save the kingdom

Elsa reaches the voice
she has been following.
She learns why she
has her power.
She finds her purpose.
She knows Anna will
find her purpose, too.

Even though Anna and Elsa
follow different paths,
their bond as sisters and friends
will always remain strong.
The love in their hearts
will hold them together forever.